For my dearest Rikka

The stories in this collection were previously published individually by
Candlewick Press, 2067 Massachusetts Avenue, Cambridge, MA 02140

Where's My Teddy? © 1992 by Jez Alborough
It's the Bear! © 1994 by Jez Alborough
My Friend Bear © 1998 by Jez Alborough

This collection copyright © 2004 by Candlewick Press

First edition in this form 2004
This edition published specially for Barnes & Noble, Inc. 2004 by Candlewick Press

2 4 6 8 10 9 7 5 3 1

Printed in China

This book was typeset in Garamond ITC.
The illustrations were done in watercolor, crayon, and pencil.

Candlewick Press
2067 Massachusetts Avenue
Cambridge, Massachusetts 02140

visit us at www.candlewick.com

WHERE'S MY TEDDY?

Jez Alborough

CANDLEWICK PRESS

CAMBRIDGE, MASSACHUSETTS

Eddie's off to find his teddy.
Eddie's teddy's name is Freddie.

He lost him in the woods somewhere.
It's dark and horrible in there.

He tiptoed
on and on
until . . .

something
made him stop
quite still.

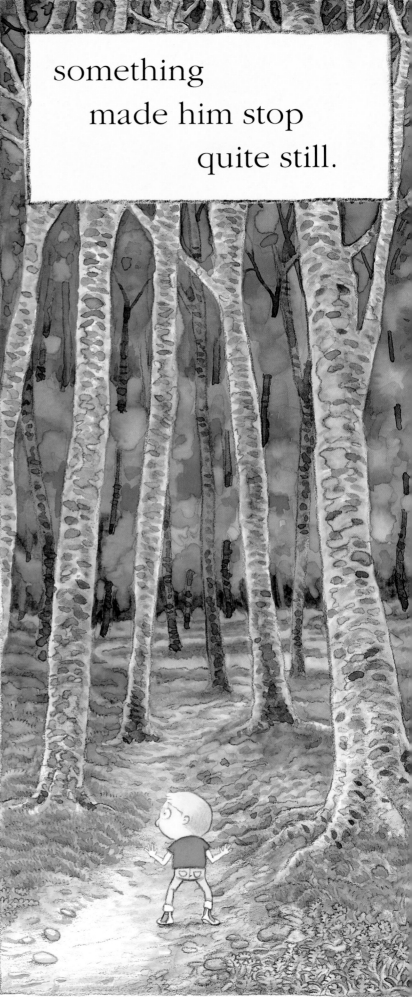

Look out! he thought. There's something there!

WHAT'S THAT?

A GIANT TEDDY BEAR!
"Is it Freddie?" said Eddie.
"What a surprise!
How *did* you get to be this size?"

"You're too big to huddle and cuddle," he said,

"and I'll never fit both of us into my bed."

Then out of the darkness,
clearer and clearer,
the sound of sobbing
came nearer and nearer.

Soon the whole woods
could hear the voice bawl,
"How did you get to be
tiny and small?
You're too small to
huddle and cuddle," it said,
"and you'll only get lost
in my giant-sized bed!"

It was a gigantic bear
and a tiny teddy
stomping toward . . .

the giant teddy and Eddie.

"MY TED!"
gasped the bear.
"A BEAR!"
screamed Eddie.

"A BOY!"
yelled the bear.
"MY TEDDY!"
cried Eddie.

Then they ran and they ran
through the dark woods
back to their homes
as fast as they could . . .

all the way back
to their snuggly beds,
where they huddled
and cuddled their
own little teds.

*For David, Amelia,
Jane, Jason and Lucy
with thanks*

IT'S THE BEAR!

Eddie doesn't want to come
and picnic in the woods with Mom.

"I'm scared," he said, "about the bear,
the great big bear that lives in there."

"A bear?" said Mom. "That's silly, dear!
We don't get great big bears around here."

"There's just you and me and your teddy, Freddie.
Now let's all get the picnic ready."

"We've got lettuce,
tomatoes, and
cream cheese spread,
with hard-boiled eggs
and crusty brown bread.
There's orange juice,
cookies,
some chips and—

OH, MY!—

I've forgotten to pack
the blueberry pie . . . "

"I'll dash back and get it," she said. "Won't be long."
"BUT MOM!"
gasped Eddie . . .

too late—
SHE HAD GONE!

He sat on the basket
and tried not to cry.
Then . . .

"I CAN SMELL FOOD!"
yelled a voice
from nearby.

"*IT'S THE BEAR,*"
cried Eddie.
"*WHERE CAN I HIDE?*"

Then he opened
the basket and
clambered inside.

Out of the trees
stepped a big hungry bear,
licking his lips
and sniffing the air.
"A teddy bear's picnic,"
he bellowed. "Hooray!"
"Help," whispered Eddie.
"He's coming this way."

He cuddled
his teddy,
he huddled
and hid. . . .

Then a great big
bear bottom

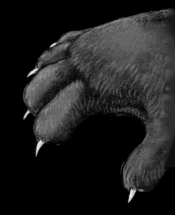

sat down on the lid.

The bear munched
and he crunched.
He chomped
and he chewed,
and greedily gobbled up
all of the food.

"*HELP!*"
shouted Eddie.

"Eddie, I'm coming," called Mom. "Are you hurt?"
"It's the bear," cried Eddie. "He thinks I'm dessert!"

"A bear?" said Mom. "I told you, my dear.
Your Freddie's the only bear around here."

To friendship

MY FRIEND BEAR

Eddie's walking with his teddy.
Eddie's teddy's name is Freddie.
"Oh, Freddie," said Eddie,
with a great big sigh.
"I feel sad, but I don't know why."
Freddie said nothing.
Eddie sighed again.
"I wish you could talk," he said.
And then . . .

"Wow! Look at that! Up there on that stone.
A giant teddy, all on his own.
We've seen him before, he belongs to the bear
who lives around these woods somewhere."

Suddenly something made Eddie turn around:
a snuffling, scuffling, bear sort of sound.
A great big voice whined, "Where's my teddy?"
"He's coming, he's coming, let's hide!" cried Eddie.

The great big bear came shuffling by,
then stopped with a sniff and started to cry.
"Oh, teddy," he whimpered, "what can I do?
I've got no friends, apart from you.
And you can't talk, and you don't care.
I'm such a sad and lonely bear."
Then, just as he brushed a tear from his eye . . .

a little voice whispered, "Please don't cry!
I'm all on my own, just like you,
with no one to talk to and nothing to do.
I'm a little bit lonely, too, you see.
If you want, you can talk to me."
The bear couldn't believe his ears.
He gulped and sniffed and wiped his tears.
"You can talk after all!" he cried.

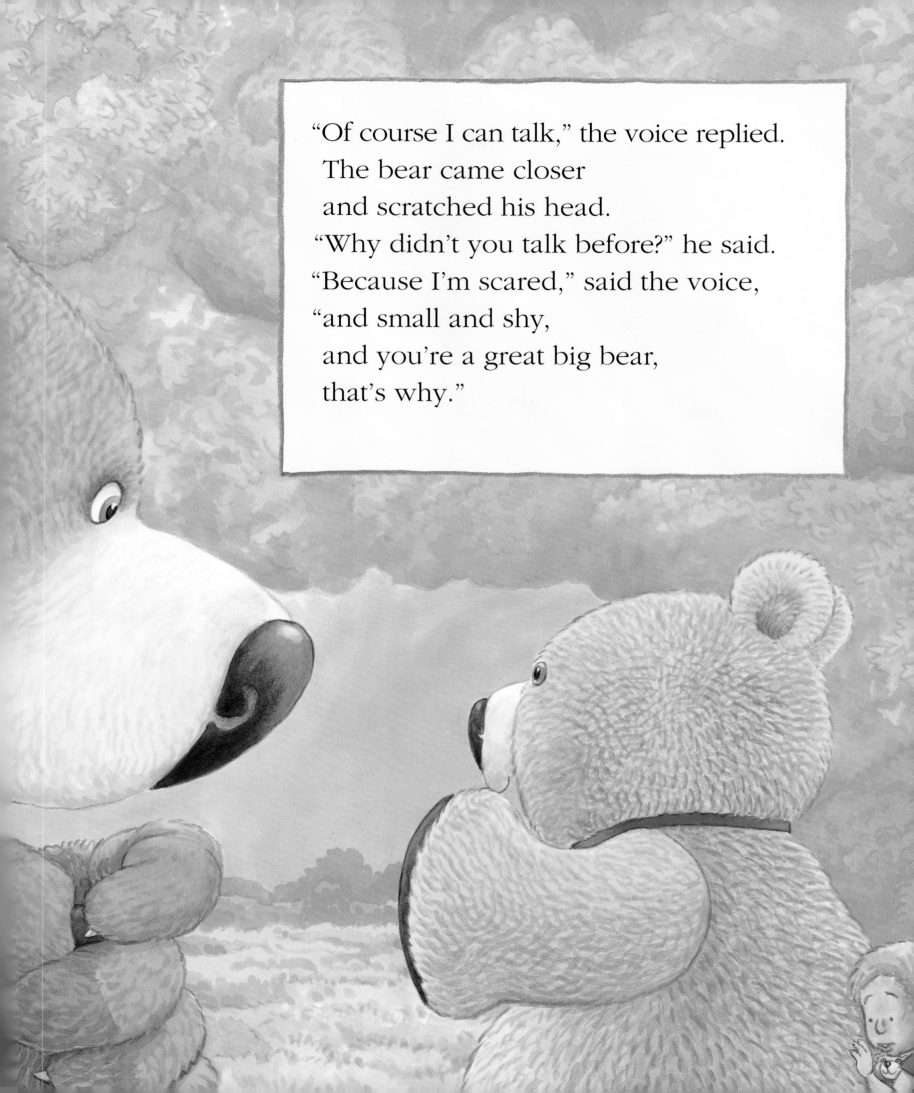

"Of course I can talk," the voice replied.
The bear came closer
and scratched his head.
"Why didn't you talk before?" he said.
"Because I'm scared," said the voice,
"and small and shy,
and you're a great big bear,
that's why."

"There, there," said the bear.
"You *are* in a muddle.
 What you need
 is a great big cuddle."
"No, I don't!" shrieked the voice.
"Yes, you do," said the bear.
"You just need some loving care.
 Don't be scared,
 you're my teddy."
"No, I'm not!" cried the voice. . . .

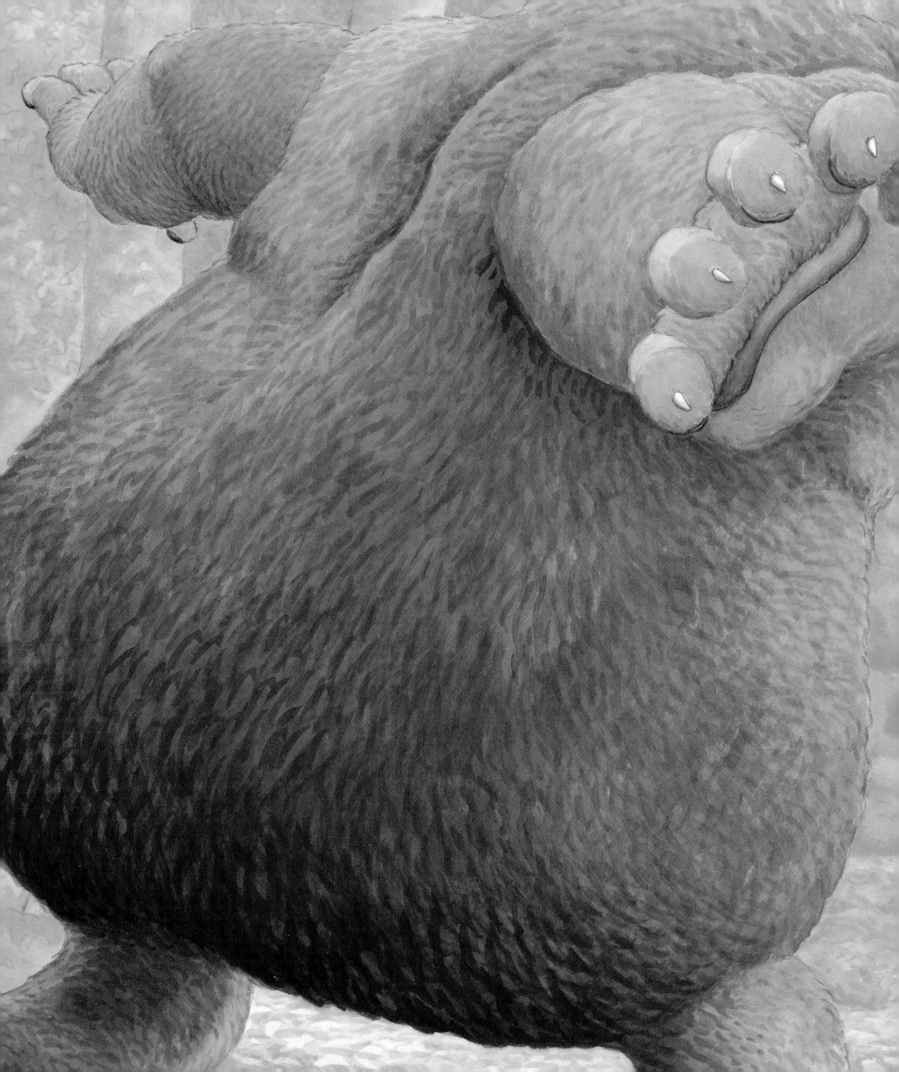

"It's me . . .

Eddie!"

The bear stared at Eddie
and clung to his teddy.
Eddie stared back
and hung on to Freddie.

Suddenly Eddie started to grin.
He felt a chuckle rise up from within.
He tried to stop it, but it wouldn't stay down.
"What's so funny?" asked the bear, with a frown.
"It's you," giggled Eddie.
"It's you, standing there.
You're such a great big silly bear!"
"No, I'm not," said the bear.
"Yes, you are!" yelped Eddie.
"You thought you had a talking teddy."

Then the bear began to snigger.
The smile on his face grew bigger and bigger.
His great big belly wiggled and jiggled.
"I am a silly bear," he giggled.
"A talking teddy—I thought it was true—
but all along it was really you."

The bear held out his giant-sized teddy,
crouched down behind it,
and said, "Hello, Eddie.
I'm a talking teddy—listen to me!
Aren't I clever? I'm only three."
Then Eddie wanted to have a go.
He held up his teddy
and squeaked, "Hello!
My name's Freddie.
How do you do?
I can talk, and
I'm only two!"

They laughed and they laughed
till their tummies were sore,
then they looked at each other
and laughed some more.
The bear started dancing and singing a song,
and he made up the words as he wobbled along.
"I'm silly," he sang, "and I don't care.
I'm such a great big silly bear!"
"Whahoo!" sang Eddie. "I'm as silly as you!
And your teddy and Freddie are silly, too."
All afternoon they played in the sun,
seeing just who was the silliest one.

When the sun began
to set in the sky,
they knew it was time
to say good-bye.

"We're friends," said Eddie.
The bear said, "Who?"
"You know," said Eddie,
"me and you."

The bear lifted Eddie
up for a hug,
hairy and beary,
safe and snug.

"Take care," he said.
"Look after Freddie!"
"We'll come back soon,"
whispered Eddie.

Then off they walked,
with a smile and a wave.
Back to a house,
and back to a cave.
Do you think that they're lonely?
Not anymore. . . .

That's what
having friends
is for.